S0-DXK-466

Caring for My Kitty

by Jane Belk Moncure
illustrated by Christina Rigo

MANKATO, MN

Library of Congress Cataloging in Publication Data

Moncure, Jane Belk.
Caring for my kitty / by Jane Belk Moncure ; illustrated by Christina Rigo.
p. cm. — (A Growing responsible book)
Summary: A little girl explains her responsibilities as she protects and takes care of her cat.
ISBN 0-89565-666-3
[1. Cats—Fiction. 2. Pets—Fiction. 3. Responsibility—Fiction.] I. Rigo, Christina Ljungren, ill. II. Title.
III. Series: Moncure, Jane Belk. Growing responsible book.
PZ7.M739Cak 1990
[E]—dc20 90-41788
CIP
AC

1 2 3 4 5 6 7 8 9 10 11 12 R 98 97 96 95 94 93 92 91

Caring for My Kitty

Kitty is so small. She needs someone to look after her. That's what I do. When she cries, I pick her up and give her a hug.

A hug is good. But Kitty needs more than a hug. When she is hungry, she needs food. It's my job to feed her every day.

CAT
FOOD

If I forget, she follows me around the house until I remember or until my mom reminds me.

Kitty needs me. That's why I stay nearby when we play outside. If she climbs too high, I can get her down.

When she gets sick, I worry about her. I take her to the vet so she can get well.

Don't Forget Your Pet's Yearly Checkup

I take care of Kitty by brushing her fur to keep it nice and pretty. She loves to be brushed.

Sometimes Kitty is lots of fun. It's fun to play games with her. And it's fun to push her in the stroller . . . except when she jumps out and runs away.

Then it's not much fun to try to find her.

And when Kitty makes a mess,
it's not much fun to clean it up.

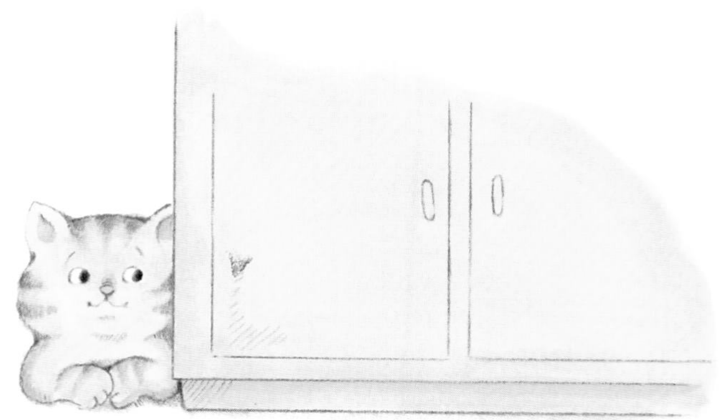

My little brother hasn't learned how to take care of Kitty. Not yet. He chases her and squeezes her.

A
B

So I teach him how to hold her gently.

Taking care of Kitty takes lots of time. I have to watch her and keep her out of trouble.

I have to keep her safe from bicycles and barking dogs.

Someday Kitty will grow up, but she will still need me. I'll always take care of her and keep her safe. Dad says she is my responsibility.

Are you a caring pet-owner? You are if you follow these five directions:

1. Always be gentle and kind to your pet.
2. Give your pet food and fresh water every day.
3. Take your pet to the vet to help it stay healthy.
4. Give your pet a clean, safe place to sleep.
5. Take time every day to play with your pet.